The HOME Team
New York Rangers®

Written by Holly Preston
Illustrated by Val Lawton

Always  Books Ltd.

The Home Team: New York Rangers®

Text and illustrations © 2014 Always Books, Ltd.
All rights reserved.

Manufactured by Friesens Corporation in Altona, MB, Canada
August 2014
Job # 204406

Library and Archives Canada Cataloguing in Publication

Preston, Holly, author
The home team : New York Rangers / written by Holly Preston ; illustrated by Val Lawton.

ISBN 978-0-9869244-7-7 (pbk.)

1. New York Rangers (Hockey team)—Juvenile fiction.
I. Lawton, Val, 1962-, illustrator II. Title.

PS8631.R467H6426 2014   jC813'.6   C2014-904485-2

Layout by Heather Nickel

MIX
Paper from
responsible sources
FSC® C016245

Always Books Ltd.
AFANFORLIFE.COM

For all young RANGERS fans
who know there's no team like ours!

There was nothing better than playing hockey …

… except watching hockey when the **NEW YORK RANGERS** played.

Ethan played defense. Jacob played forward. Michael was in goal.
The boys played different positions. They had the same dream:
to one day play for the **NEW YORK RANGERS**.

Even after playing all day, Jacob dreamed only about hockey.

The only problem was Jacob never scored. Ever.

The puck went high. The puck went low.

The puck went everywhere but where it was supposed to go.

How can I ever become one of the **NEW YORK RANGERS**? Jacob wondered.

His sister Mia was the best goal scorer in the neighborhood.

"The **RANGERS** were little boys once, too, Jacob," his dad said.
"They didn't become hockey stars overnight.

His mom said, "You can learn a lot by watching what the **RANGERS** do."
She'd been a **RANGERS** fan forever.

The **RANGERS** are great skaters.

They make big plays.

They shoot. They score!

And make a million saves.

"The only way to get better is to practice," said Ethan.

And so they practiced hard. And then came the best surprise they'd ever had.

"We're going to a **RANGERS** game!" Michael yelled.

But at the game, the **RANGERS** top scorer wasn't scoring at all!

"Something is wrong," said Jacob.

The next day on the way to the rink, Jacob found a shiny chain.

He put it on and … he got a goal! And then another one!

"That's a good luck charm, for sure," Mia said.

"Our player lost his good luck charm, kids," said Dad. "Maybe *that's* why he hasn't been scoring." The children knew hockey players were superstitious. They also knew where that charm was …

And what they had to do next!

Jacob seized the moment.
"What does it take to play for the **NEW YORK RANGERS**?" he asked.

Play like a team…

...and with heart.

Never give up.

Believe in yourself.

"The **RANGERS** are the greatest team in the NHL," said Ethan.

"We're going to be **RANGERS** fans forever," added Michael.

Everything was the way it should be.

All the next week Jacob practiced and practiced.
He no longer had the good luck charm, but he had something else—
he believed in himself.

And that was all he really needed.

But Jacob, like all hockey players, knew a little luck always helps…

...especially when you're playing for the Stanley Cup®!

ABOUT THE AUTHOR
Holly Preston

Holly Preston is a journalist who worked for CTV and CBC. She grew up watching NHL hockey with her brother and father. Now she creates children's picture books for professional sports teams. She hopes Rangers fans will enjoy having a book that celebrates their home team and encourages young fans to find a love of reading.

ABOUT THE ILLUSTRATOR
Val Lawton

Val Lawton is an artist, an artist-educator with the Learning Through the Arts Program, and a children's book illustrator. The Home Team: New York Rangers *is her 27th book.*